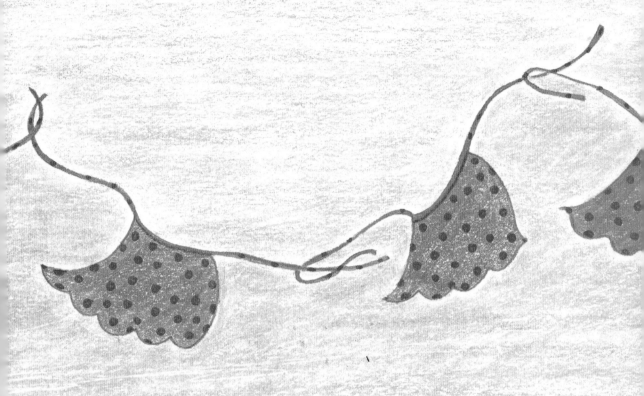

To my dear father,

who knew how to calm the storm

—L. J.

For cutie pie

—P. M.

Text copyright © 2001 by Lynne Jonell
Illustrations copyright © 2001 by Petra Mathers
G. P. Putnam's Sons, a division of
Penguin Putnam Books for Young Readers,
345 Hudson Street, New York, NY 10014.
G. P. Putnam's Sons, Reg. U.S. Pat. & Tm. Off.
Published simultaneously in Canada.
Printed in Hong Kong by South China Printing Co. (1988) Ltd.
Designed by Sharon Jacobs. Text set in fourteen point Catchup.
Library of Congress Cataloging-in-Publication Data
Jonell, Lynne. Mom pie / Lynne Jonell; illustrated by Petra Mathers. p.cm.
Summary: Because their mother seems too busy preparing for company,
Christopher and Robbie cook up the idea of a Mom pie to serve as her surrogate.
[1. Mothers—Fiction. 2. Mother and child—Fiction.] I. Mathers, Petra, ill. II. Title.
PZ7.J675Mog 2001 [E]—dc21 99-24005 CIP
ISBN 0-399-23422-5
1 3 5 7 9 10 8 6 4 2
FIRST IMPRESSION

Mom Pie

Written by Lynne Jonell

Illustrated by Petra Mathers

G. P. PUTNAM'S SONS ~ NEW YORK

Mommy was very busy.
"The potatoes are boiling over!
I have to baste the turkey!
Oh, no! I forgot to order flowers!"

Mommy sent Daddy to the store with a list.
Then she ran to the stove
and stirred something very fast.
"I can help stir," Christopher said.
Mommy did not answer.

"I can stir, too," said Robbie. "I have a dish."
Mommy shook something in a bottle.
"You will help me best if you
stay out of the kitchen," she said.

Christopher backed away.

He bumped into Robbie.

"Ouch!"

"Mommy, Robbie hurt his knee!"
Mommy did not turn around. "Is it bleeding?"
"No."
"Well, put a Band-Aid on it and go somewhere
else to play. I have a lot to do."

Christopher walked out slowly. Robbie followed.

"Why is Mommy too busy?" Robbie asked.

"Because company is coming," said Christopher.

"I don't like company," said Robbie.

"You will like the food," said Christopher.

"And we are having three kinds of pie."

"But we are not having Mommy," said Robbie.

"I don't like any kind of pie without Mommy."

"We could make a Mom pie," said Christopher.
"You would like that kind of pie, I bet."
Robbie looked at his dish.
"Would it hurt Mommy to be in a pie?"

"Not very much," said Christopher.

"Not if we just used little bits of Mommy."

"Here is a little bit," said Robbie.

"It is soft and smooth like Mommy."

"Good," said Christopher.

"And here is something snuggly."

"But not as snuggly as Mommy," said Robbie.

"I know," said Christopher.

"We'll just take them to remind us."

"We can put in her earring.
And here is her perfume."
Christopher opened the bottle.
"It smells like Mommy," said Robbie.

"We need one more thing," said Christopher.

"Her favorite color."

"It is too big for the dish," said Robbie.

"Not now," said Christopher.

"Are we done?" asked Robbie.

"Yes," said Christopher. "Now we stir it all together.
And then we put it on the table."

"We helped!" said Robbie.

"What have you done?" cried Mommy.

"We made Mom pie," said Christopher.

"It is the best kind," said Robbie.

Mommy sat down.

"I do not understand," she said.

"Did you want to eat Mom pie?"

"Mom pie is not good to eat," said Christopher.

"It is good to touch and to smell."

"And to snuggle with," said Robbie,

"when you are too busy."

The door opened.

In came Daddy with his arms full.

In came the company, talking all at once.

"Welcome!" said Mommy. But she did not get up.

Aunt Teresa went to mash the potatoes.
Grandma Sam arranged the flowers. Uncle Paul
carried chairs, and Daddy carved the turkey.
"Is it all done?" asked Daddy. "Are we ready for dinner?"

"All but the candle," said Mommy,

"and I have help for that."

Robbie held the candle. Christopher fixed it.

And Mommy put it back on the table.

"There!" she said. "Now we are ready to eat.
Isn't this better than Mom pie?"

"Nothing is better than Mom pie," said Christopher.

"Except a Mom," said Robbie.